LOVE, MURDER AND MYSTERY

"True love is what endures even in silence, lying beside memory's coffin, undisturbed, unwavering—proof that even death cannot bury devotion."

By Sahil Shah

INTRODUCTION

In a city where shadows breathe and silence holds secrets, unfolds the story of Joey and Janet—a love so powerful that even death could not silence it.

What begins as a tender romance of stolen glances and whispered promises soon spirals into a world of betrayal, unanswered questions, and a crime that will leave blood on the canvas of their love.

But love is not bound by time or tragedy. When the last chapter closes on earth, another begins in heaven, where two souls discover that eternity belongs to them.

This is not merely a tale of passion. It is a story of devotion tested by mystery, of romance entwined with suspense, and of love's triumph over mortality itself.

SUMMARY

Love, Murder and Mystery follows Joey and Janet through twelve chapters of passion, suspense, and fate.

Their romance blossoms in secrecy, hidden behind smiles that carry untold truths. As their connection deepens, so too does the darkness surrounding them. Letters left unsent, a haunting voicemail, a man lurking in the shadows—all become threads in a web that tightens until it ends in a chilling crime scene.

Yet even in death, their story does not fade. In a final, breathtaking chapter, Joey and Janet are reunited in heaven, proving that love remembers what life forgets.

Chapter Titles:

1. The Beginning of Us
2. Stolen Moments
3. Secrets Behind Her Smile
4. Blood on the Canvas

CHAPTER 1: THE BEGINNING OF US

The café smelled of roasted beans and warm vanilla, the kind of scent that wrapped itself around you like an embrace. Joey sat in the corner, his notebook open before him, though he hadn't written a single line. His pen rested idly in his hand, tapping against the page as his mind wandered.

Outside the tall windows, the city was alive in its usual way—taxi horns, voices layered over the hum of traffic, the soft rhythm of a street musician's guitar echoing down the block. But inside, in that pocket of warmth and steam, Joey felt detached, suspended in a quiet space where the world could pass him by.

He came here often, usually with the intent to write. Music, mostly. Fragments of songs that never seemed to find their endings. Once, he had believed he would compose something that mattered, something that could outlast him. Lately, though, the notes slipped away like smoke, vanishing before they could take form.

And then he saw her.

At first, it was nothing more than a glance—his eyes drifting up from his empty page to the window where she sat. But that single glance felt like stepping off a ledge into something bottomless.

She sat alone, a book open in her lap, sunlight from the late afternoon streaming through the glass behind her. It touched her hair, catching strands of chestnut and gold, and softened the edges of her profile. She wasn't trying to be noticed—her clothes were simple, her posture unassuming—but Joey noticed her all the same.

Her lips curved faintly, as though the words on the page whispered secrets meant only for her. There was an ease in the way she existed, as if she had long ago made peace with the world's chaos. But there was something else too, something in the quiet weight of her eyes that hinted at stories untold.

Joey's pen stilled. The world, in that moment, seemed to quiet around him. He became aware of his own heartbeat, loud and insistent, echoing in the silence he hadn't realized was there.

For a long moment, he simply watched. Not staring, he told himself—observing. But when she lifted her gaze from the book, when her eyes met his across the room, he knew he had been caught.

The air shifted.

It was nothing dramatic—no lightning, no music swelling from invisible strings—but it was undeniable. Recognition. That was the only word he could find. As if two lives, until now running parallel, had suddenly converged.

She smiled, small and deliberate. It wasn't the kind of smile you gave a stranger. It was the kind you gave someone who mattered.

Joey forgot to breathe.

Minutes passed, or maybe seconds. He couldn't tell. But before doubt could creep in, before fear could tie his tongue, he closed his notebook, rose from his seat, and crossed the room.

When he stopped by her table, his voice betrayed him, quieter than intended. "What are you reading?"

Her hands, delicate but sure, tilted the book so he could see the cover: Wuthering Heights.

Joey blinked, trying to summon something intelligent to say. Of all the books, it had to be that one. Love twisted into obsession, passion carved into tragedy. A story that didn't end happily.

"Love and tragedy," she said, her voice carrying a lilt, smooth and unhurried. "The kind of story that lingers."

Something in the way she said it told Joey she wasn't just talking about the book.

He smiled, though his throat was dry. "Maybe the kind of story worth living."

Her eyes flickered with interest. A test, perhaps. Then she closed the book, slid it aside, and gestured at the empty chair across from her.

"Sit," she said.

And Joey did.

The hours melted, unnoticed. At first, their words were cautious, polite, but soon they flowed with surprising ease. Janet spoke of books she'd loved since childhood, of letters she wrote but never sent, words poured onto pages that no one would ever read. Joey admitted he once believed music would save him, that he wrote songs like prayers, though he hadn't touched a piano in years.

It startled him, how much he told her. Secrets that felt too heavy for others, he placed in her hands without hesitation. She received them gently, as if she understood.

Sometimes she laughed—really laughed—and the sound lingered, filling the spaces inside him that had been empty for too long. Other times, she fell quiet, her gaze drifting, her smile turning into something softer, sadder. Joey noticed but didn't ask. He didn't want to break the spell.

When the café closed and the barista stacked chairs on tables, neither of them had moved to leave. Time had vanished.

Finally, as they stood on the sidewalk outside, Joey felt panic stir. The night air was cool, the city buzzing with neon and noise, but all he could think was: What if I never see her again?

Janet, however, seemed untroubled. She tilted her head, studying him like she was memorizing the lines of his face. Then, with a quiet certainty, she said, "Same time tomorrow?"

And just like that, fear dissolved.

Joey smiled—really smiled, the kind he hadn't worn in years. "Tomorrow," he echoed, as if it were a vow.

Sleep never came easily to Joey, but that night, it felt like an impossibility. He tossed and turned, sheets twisting around his legs, staring at the cracks in his ceiling like they might spell out answers.

Her face appeared every time he closed his eyes—the way she brushed her hair back, the way she leaned in when something fascinated her, the quiet strength in her voice when she spoke of books and unsent letters. He thought of her smile, and then of the shadow beneath it, something unspoken.

By three in the morning, he gave up on rest altogether. He got up, padded barefoot to his old piano, and lifted the fallboard. The keys were dusty, untouched for weeks, maybe months. His fingers hovered, hesitant, then pressed down gently. A simple chord, one he'd played a thousand times, but tonight it resonated differently.

He closed his eyes, and the music began to form—not whole, not finished, but something raw. Something that carried the memory of her laugh, the weight of her gaze. For the first time in years, notes didn't feel empty. They felt alive.

When dawn finally broke, Joey sat slumped against the piano, his notebook now filled with scribbled fragments of melody. He smiled faintly to himself. Music had returned, carried back on the memory of a woman he'd just met.

The next day at the café, Joey arrived early. Too early. He sat at the same corner table, fingers drumming against his cup as he tried to appear casual. His notebook lay open in front of him, though he barely looked at it. Every sound—the chime of the door, the shuffle of feet—sent a ripple of anticipation through him.

When Janet walked in, it was like the room shifted again, tilting just slightly in her direction.

She didn't look surprised to see him. Instead, she smiled—softly, knowingly—as if she'd expected it all along. She carried another book, its spine worn, its pages marked with tiny folded corners. She slid into the seat across from him without asking, her presence filling the space as naturally as breath.

"You came early," she said.

"Couldn't sleep," Joey admitted before he could stop himself.

Her eyebrows lifted slightly, amused. "Insomnia, or something else?"

"Something else," he said, and though he didn't elaborate, her smile told him she understood anyway.

Their conversation that afternoon meandered like a river, slow and steady. Janet spoke of her childhood—nights spent in libraries, tracing words with her finger until they imprinted on her. Joey shared stories of sneaking into empty concert halls as a teenager, pressing keys just to hear echoes fill the silence.

Sometimes they laughed. Other times, silence stretched between them, comfortable rather than awkward. Joey found himself studying her in those quiet moments: the way she tapped her fingers against her mug when deep in thought, the way her gaze seemed to drift far beyond the café walls, as if she were listening to echoes he couldn't hear.

At one point, she caught him staring. "You watch people," she said softly.

"Maybe," Joey replied. "Or maybe I'm just watching you."

Her cheeks flushed faintly, but she didn't look away.

As the days turned into weeks, the café became theirs. A place carved out of routine, a world that belonged only to them. The barista began to recognize them as a pair, often smiling knowingly as she set down their drinks without waiting for orders.

Joey noticed the little things. Janet always carried a pen tucked behind her ear, as if ready to write at any moment. She never used sugar in her coffee. When she laughed, she sometimes pressed her hand to her chest, as though to steady her heart.

And Janet noticed him too. She teased him about the way he furrowed his brow when thinking, the way his fingers drummed against tabletops as though searching for rhythm.

One afternoon, she leaned across the table, her eyes curious. "What are you afraid of, Joey?"

The question caught him off guard. He almost deflected with humor, but something about her gaze—steady, unwavering—made him answer honestly.

"Being forgotten," he said quietly.

Her expression softened. "You won't be."

He wanted to believe her.

The first time they touched was accidental. Their hands brushed as they both reached for a napkin, fingers grazing. The contact was brief, but it jolted through Joey like electricity. Janet froze, then slowly drew her hand back. She didn't look away, though. She held his gaze, and something unspoken passed between them.

After that, the touches came more easily. Her hand on his arm when she laughed, his fingers brushing hers as they walked out into the night. Small moments, fleeting yet monumental.

Joey didn't dare name what was happening. Naming it felt like it might shatter. But deep down, he knew: something had begun that neither of them could stop.

One evening, as twilight painted the city in gold and violet, they walked along the river. The water shimmered, catching the glow of streetlights. Janet's hand brushed his, lingered, then intertwined with his fingers. She didn't say anything. She didn't have to.

Joey's chest ached with the simplicity of it, the rightness of it. He had never believed in fate. He wasn't sure he did even now. But in that moment, with Janet's hand in his, it felt like the universe had been leading him here all along.

Later, when Joey returned home, he opened his notebook again. But this time, he didn't struggle. The words came easily, the music flowing with them.

For the first time in years, the page filled.

And he knew—it wasn't just music anymore. It was Janet.

The beginning of us.

CHAPTER 2: STOLEN MOMENTS

The days after that river walk felt like they belonged to someone else's life. Joey found himself moving through the city with a quiet buoyancy, like a man who had stumbled into a secret he could not yet explain. Every morning, the gray buildings looked less oppressive, the streets less chaotic. Even the air tasted different.

And always, at the heart of it, was Janet.

She wasn't just in his thoughts—she was in his routines now. They had built a rhythm without realizing it. Coffee in the late afternoons, conversations that spilled into evenings, and sometimes, when the city had gone quiet and the café lights dimmed, walks through narrow lanes or along the riverbank.

Yet for all the time they shared, Joey felt it slipping too quickly through his fingers, as though he were racing against something invisible. That urgency gave their moments together an intensity that neither of them named but both of them felt.

It was a Wednesday afternoon when he first realized how much she had changed him. Joey had been scheduled to meet an old friend for lunch, but after only half an hour, he found his mind wandering, restless, waiting for the hour when he could walk into the café and find her sitting by the window.

When he finally did, there she was—head bent over another book, this time a collection of poetry, her fingers absentmindedly tracing the rim of her cup. She looked up at the sound of his approach, and the corners of her lips curved into that familiar, knowing smile.

"You look distracted," she teased, setting the book aside.

"Maybe I am." Joey sat across from her. "What are you reading this time?"

She slid the book across the table. Pablo Neruda: Love Poems.

He raised his eyebrows, trying to mask the sudden quickening of his heart. "That's… not exactly light reading."

Her smile deepened, almost mischievous. "Do you believe words can make someone fall in love?"

The question hung in the air between them, bold and disarming. Joey felt the heat crawl up his neck, but he forced himself to meet her gaze.

"I think," he said slowly, "words can make someone remember what love feels like. Maybe that's the same thing."

Her eyes lingered on his for a moment, as if she were weighing his honesty, before she looked away, brushing her hair back from her face. "Good answer."

It was in those exchanges—half-teasing, half-revealing—that Joey began to understand what made Janet different. She didn't settle for shallow conversation. She asked questions that went straight to the bone, questions that left you exposed but strangely grateful.

"Why did you stop playing music?" she asked one evening, as they walked along a crowded street lined with glowing shop windows.

He hesitated. The easy answer was failure, or perhaps fear. But with Janet, the easy answer never felt enough.

"Because I forgot what it felt like," he admitted finally. "I used to believe every note mattered. That music could change things. But somewhere along the way, I stopped believing that. And once I stopped, the music disappeared."

Janet walked in silence beside him, her hand brushing his as if testing the waters. "And now?" she asked softly.

Joey turned his head toward her. The neon lights painted her face in shifting colors, her expression unreadable. "Now…" His throat tightened. "Now I hear it again."

Her hand lingered against his this time, their fingers almost intertwining before she pulled back. "Good," she whispered.

Their stolen moments began to multiply. A lingering glance across the café. A brush of hands as they reached for the same cup. A walk that ended too late, where parting felt like a kind of theft.

One evening, it rained. Not a drizzle, but a downpour, sheets of water pounding against the pavement. The café was nearly empty, the world outside blurred into streaks of light and shadow. Joey and Janet sat close, shoulders nearly touching, watching raindrops race each other down the window.

"I love the rain," Janet said suddenly, her voice softer than usual.

"Why?"

"Because it hides everything. You can cry, and no one knows. You can kiss someone in the street, and it feels like the whole world is washing itself away."

Joey's heart stuttered at the thought, though he kept his eyes on the window. "So… would you?"

She turned to him, her expression unreadable. "Would I what?"

"Kiss someone in the rain."

The silence stretched, thick with possibility. Finally, she smiled faintly, almost wistfully. "Maybe, if the moment was right."

Joey didn't push further, though every fiber of his being wanted to. Instead, he let the moment pass, storing her words like a secret melody.

By now, the city had stopped feeling like his. It was theirs. Every corner seemed to carry a memory—the café where they first spoke, the bookstore where she dragged him to find her favorite authors, the narrow alley where he once made her laugh so hard she doubled over, clutching his arm.

But it wasn't just the city that was changing. It was Joey himself. He noticed the way he leaned into the world now, no longer retreating into solitude. Music came easier. Words filled his notebooks again. And when he thought of the future, it no longer stretched out as an empty corridor.

One night, as they sat on a bench overlooking the river, Janet leaned back, her hair falling loosely over her shoulders. "Do you ever feel like we're borrowing time?" she asked.

The question startled him. "What do you mean?"

Her gaze was fixed on the dark water. "Like we're stealing moments we're not supposed to have. That somewhere, someone is keeping count, and one day they'll come to collect."

Joey studied her profile, the curve of her cheek, the glimmer of light in her eyes. "If that's true," he said quietly, "then let's steal as many as we can."

She turned to him then, and for a heartbeat, it felt as though she might close the distance between them. But she didn't. Instead, she smiled—softly, sadly—and looked back at the water.

Joey didn't press. But inside, something ached.

As the weeks deepened into months, their connection became undeniable. Friends noticed Joey's absence, his tendency to disappear for hours at a time. He didn't explain. How could he? How could he put into words the way Janet's presence had rewired his world?

Yet, even in their closeness, there were walls. Janet was a mystery he could not entirely unravel. She would laugh and tease and share stories, but then, without warning, she would retreat behind silence, her eyes distant, as though listening to something only she could hear.

Once, late at night, she confessed: "I write letters. To people I've lost. To people I'll never send them to."

"Why?" Joey asked.

"Because sometimes words are safer when they're trapped on paper."

He wanted to ask if one of those letters was for him, but he didn't. He wasn't ready for the answer.

The first time they kissed, it wasn't in the rain or beneath some poetic sunset. It was in the quiet corner of the café, long after most of the customers had left. Janet was reading aloud from a book of Neruda, her voice low and melodic. Joey wasn't listening to the words—he was listening to her.

When she paused to sip her coffee, he leaned in before he could lose his nerve. Their lips met, tentative at first, then deeper, lingering. The world didn't vanish, but it blurred.

When they pulled apart, Janet's eyes searched his. "That was—" she began.

"Stolen," Joey finished.

She smiled, her forehead resting briefly against his. "Then let's keep stealing."

And they did. Again and again.

Every moment with her became a treasure, but also a risk. Joey knew it. He could feel it in the way she sometimes looked away, in the weight of her unspoken words. But he ignored the fear. He told himself stories of forever, even as a small voice whispered that forever was fragile.

Because in the end, what mattered was simple:

Janet was his stolen moment.

And he was hers.

CHAPTER 3: SECRETS BEHIND HER SMILE

Janet's smile had always been a puzzle.

At first, Joey thought it was simply radiant—soft, inviting, a smile that lit up the corners of a room without trying. But as their days together stretched into weeks, he realized something more. It wasn't just warmth that her smile carried; it was weight. Behind every curve of her lips, there lingered a shadow.

He began to notice the small details.

When she laughed, her hand sometimes covered her mouth, as if concealing something too fragile to be exposed. When someone asked her a question that grazed too close to her past, her smile would appear almost instantly, a mask sliding into place. And when she sat in silence, lost in thought, her lips would press together in the faintest line—no joy, no ease, just the echo of something unsaid.

It unsettled Joey. But it also drew him in. He wanted to know what lived behind that smile, what stories it hid.

One evening, as they lingered in the café long after their cups had gone cold, Joey reached across the table, his fingers brushing hers.

"Tell me something real," he said.

Her brow furrowed, playful at first. "Everything I tell you is real."

"You know what I mean." His voice softened. "Tell me something you don't say out loud. Something behind the smile."

Janet looked at him for a long moment, her eyes unreadable. Then she leaned back, her fingers slipping away from his. "Careful what you ask for, Joey."

"I'm not afraid," he said, though part of him was.

She let out a quiet laugh, but it wasn't amusement. It was closer to resignation. "You should be."

And then, as quickly as the moment came, she changed the subject, asking about his music, his day, anything else. The wall had returned, and Joey, though frustrated, let it stand.

That night, lying awake, he thought of her words. You should be.

Was it a warning? A confession? He couldn't shake the chill it left behind.

But the next day, when she greeted him with her familiar smile, he pushed the doubts aside. Because when Janet looked at him, when her hand slipped into his, everything felt right. And Joey wasn't ready to question that.

Weeks passed. Their intimacy grew, deepened. They spent hours wandering through the city, discovering hidden corners and forgotten streets. Janet had a way of turning the ordinary into magic—an abandoned building became a canvas for stories, a cracked sidewalk became a stage for laughter.

Yet even in their closeness, the distance remained. Joey noticed how she avoided certain questions: her family, her past relationships, where she disappeared to on nights she didn't answer his calls.

Once, he asked where she'd been the night before. She smiled, pressed a finger to his lips, and whispered, "Not tonight."

It was intoxicating and maddening all at once.

One evening, Joey invited her to his apartment. It was small, cluttered with books and sheet music, but he wanted her to see his world beyond the café and the streets.

She walked slowly through the space, fingertips grazing the edges of his piano, pausing at the stack of notebooks filled with half-written songs.

"You keep everything," she murmured.

"Even the unfinished things matter," Joey said.

Her eyes lingered on him then, something heavy in her gaze. "Not everything unfinished deserves to stay."

Before he could ask what she meant, she kissed him. It was sudden, almost desperate, as though she wanted to silence her own thoughts. Joey pulled her close, the world narrowing to the taste of her lips, the weight of her body against his.

When they finally broke apart, she pressed her forehead to his, whispering, "Promise me something."

"Anything," he breathed.

"Don't try to fix me."

Joey froze. He wanted to tell her she wasn't broken, that she didn't need fixing. But the words caught in his throat. Because deep down, he wondered if she believed it too much for him to change her mind.

Their nights together became heavier after that. Passionate, yes, but laced with something else—urgency, fragility, as if every touch might be the last. Joey began to notice how Janet sometimes pulled away after intimacy, curling into herself, her back turned, her body trembling as though fighting off ghosts.

Once, in the dim light, he reached for her hand. "Talk to me," he whispered.

Her voice was so faint he barely heard it. "If I tell you, you'll leave."

"Never."

She looked at him then, her smile sad, broken at the edges. "Don't make promises you can't keep."

Joey kissed her forehead, but inside, a storm was building.

The secrets began to spill, not all at once, but in fragments, whispered between moments.

She told him about the letters she wrote at night, addressed to people she would never send them to. She admitted she sometimes stood on her balcony at three in the morning, staring down at the street, wondering how easy it would be to let go. She confessed that love terrified her more than loneliness, because it made her vulnerable, because it could be taken away.

Each confession was followed by a smile, as though she could erase the weight of her words with that curve of her lips. But Joey saw through it now. He saw the cracks, the fissures running deep beneath her calm exterior.

And though he loved her more fiercely for it, fear took root in him. Fear of losing her, fear of not being enough to hold her together.

One night, he woke to find her standing by his window, the city lights painting her in silver.

"What are you doing?" he asked, his voice groggy.

"Listening," she said.

"To what?"

"To the silence between the sounds." She turned, her eyes glistening. "It's louder than people realize."

He got up, wrapped his arms around her from behind, pressed his cheek against her hair. "You don't have to carry it alone."

Her smile appeared again, fragile and fleeting. "I've always carried it alone, Joey."

But she leaned into him all the same.

The more Joey tried to reach her, the more he realized how deep her shadows went. And yet, he couldn't turn away. Because in every moment of light she gave him—in every laugh, every stolen glance, every kiss that felt like fire—he felt alive in a way he hadn't in years.

Janet was both the wound and the healing.

And Joey, despite the warnings, was already too far gone.

When she smiled at him across the café the next day, the same smile that had first drawn him in, Joey knew the truth at last.

Behind that smile lived secrets he might never fully know.

But he also knew this: he would spend whatever time he had trying to understand them.

Trying to understand her.

CHAPTER 4: BLOOD ON THE CANVAS

The gallery smelled faintly of turpentine and varnish, a perfume of creation and decay. Joey had never been much of a painter, but he loved watching Janet move through the space. She drifted between canvases like she belonged there, her eyes tracing every stroke, her fingers hovering as if she could feel the heartbeat of the art without touching it.

"This one," she said, stopping before a massive canvas splattered with crimson streaks and shadows of black. "It looks like rage, doesn't it?"

Joey tilted his head. "Or grief."

Janet smiled faintly, though her eyes didn't leave the canvas. "Maybe both."

They stood in silence, staring. To Joey, the painting looked violent, chaotic. To Janet, it seemed to be something else entirely. Her hand tightened around his as if bracing herself.

"Do you ever wonder," she murmured, "if artists leave pieces of themselves behind? That every brushstroke, every note, is a confession they can't make with words?"

Joey glanced at her, the way the gallery's soft light traced her cheekbones. "I think that's the only reason art exists."

Janet's lips parted slightly, as if she wanted to say something else, but instead she let out a shaky laugh. "Maybe that's why it scares me."

The gallery had invited Joey because one of his old acquaintances—a painter named Elias—was hosting a private exhibition. Joey hadn't spoken to Elias in years, not since the days when their youthful arrogance clashed over women, ambition, and the idea of success.

But Janet had insisted. "You need to step back into the world," she told him. "Let's do this together."

So here they were, standing amidst canvases that bled emotion. Joey wasn't sure if it was courage or masochism that kept him here, but with Janet by his side, he felt steadier.

Until Elias appeared.

"Joey. I didn't think you'd actually show." Elias's voice was smooth, too smooth, his smile cutting. He wore a tailored jacket splattered just enough with paint to appear authentic.

"Elias," Joey said flatly.

Janet glanced between them, sensing the tension immediately. She extended her hand politely. "Janet."

Elias took it, his gaze lingering a beat too long. "A pleasure. You've brought light into his shadow, I see."

Joey bristled, but Janet only offered a small smile before slipping her hand back into Joey's.

As the evening wore on, the gallery filled with the hum of conversation and the clink of glasses. Joey tried to focus on the art, on Janet, but his unease grew. Elias's eyes followed them, watching, calculating.

At one point, Janet excused herself to the restroom. Elias seized the moment, stepping close enough for Joey to smell the faint mix of paint and cologne.

"She's beautiful," Elias said, his tone casual but his eyes sharp. "But you know beauty doesn't last, Joey. Not in your hands."

Joey's fists clenched. "Stay out of it."

Elias's smirk widened. "Just remember—blood and love mix easily on the canvas."

Joey turned away, forcing himself to breathe, to not cause a scene. But the words lodged deep, festering.

When Janet returned, her hand slipped into his again. She noticed his tension, the tightness in his jaw. "What happened?"

"Nothing," he lied. "Just old ghosts."

But Janet's eyes searched his, and for a moment he thought she might press further. Instead, she only squeezed his hand and whispered, "Don't let the ghosts win."

Later that night, back at Joey's apartment, Janet sat cross-legged on the floor surrounded by his notebooks. She flipped through them slowly, tracing the ink with her fingers.

"These are you," she whispered. "Every unfinished song, every broken line. You've been bleeding on these pages for years."

Joey knelt beside her, his chest tightening. "And you? Where do you bleed?"

Her eyes lifted, shimmering in the dim light. "On paper. In silence. In ways you'll never fully see."

Joey cupped her face, kissed her deeply, trying to erase the distance. But when they broke apart, he tasted salt. She had been crying without a sound.

The nightmares began soon after.

Joey would wake in the middle of the night to find Janet restless, thrashing, whispering words he couldn't understand. Once, she gasped awake, her hands clawing at her chest as though fighting for air.

"Janet!" He pulled her into his arms, her body trembling violently. "It's just a dream."

Her eyes were wild, distant. "No," she whispered. "It's not just a dream."

He held her until her breathing slowed, but the chill never left him.

The next morning, she smiled as though nothing had happened. But Joey couldn't forget. The image of crimson on canvas, Elias's taunt, Janet's silent tears—they began to blur together into something ominous.

Their stolen moments grew more desperate, more urgent. Every kiss felt like a confession, every touch like a plea. Joey wanted to believe love could save them both, but the shadows in Janet's smile told him otherwise.

One evening, as the sun dipped below the horizon, Joey sat at the piano while Janet leaned against the window. He played softly, the notes fragile, unfinished.

Janet turned, her eyes distant. "If something happened to me… would you still play?"

The question cut through him. "Don't say that."

"Promise me," she pressed, her voice trembling. "Promise me you'll keep playing, no matter what."

Joey's throat tightened. "Janet—"

"Promise me," she repeated, tears brimming now, her smile trembling at the edges.

"I promise," he whispered, though the words tasted like ash.

She closed her eyes, a single tear trailing down her cheek. And then she smiled again, that same haunting smile that had both saved him and broken him from the very beginning.

That night, Joey dreamt of the gallery again. Of crimson streaks across the canvas. Of Elias's smirk. And of Janet, her smile fading into blood.

When he woke, the echo of her voice lingered: Promise me.

And for the first time, Joey wondered if love alone could keep them safe.

CHAPTER 5: LETTERS SHE NEVER SENT

Janet had always been careful with her words. In conversation, she chose them like a painter chose colors—deliberately, with intention, each one carrying weight. But Joey learned that her real words, her deepest ones, didn't live in their talks at the café or whispered exchanges in the dark.

They lived on paper.

It started one rainy evening when she invited him to her apartment for the first time. The space was small, scattered with plants that leaned toward the light of the tall windows. A faint scent of lavender hung in the air, soothing but tinged with melancholy. Books were stacked everywhere—by the couch, on the windowsill, in uneven piles on the floor.

Joey loved it immediately. It felt like her.

While she moved to make tea, Joey wandered, careful not to disturb her things. That was when he saw the stack of envelopes, neatly tied with twine, resting on a corner of her desk. Each one bore a date in the corner, but no names.

When Janet returned, he gestured toward them. "Letters?"

Her eyes flickered, almost imperceptibly. "Yes."

"To who?"

She set the cups down and sat across from him, her shoulders tense. "To no one. To everyone. To people I've lost. To versions of myself I'll never be again. To ghosts."

Joey hesitated. "Do you send them?"

Her laugh was soft, humorless. "No. That's the point. They're not meant to be read."

But later, as the evening wore on and the tea cooled between them, she surprised him.

"Do you want to see one?" she asked quietly.

Joey met her gaze, uncertain. "Only if you want me to."

She rose, untied the twine, and chose an envelope near the middle of the stack. She didn't let him touch it. Instead, she unfolded the page herself and read aloud.

Her voice trembled, but her words were steady.

"To the one I never got to say goodbye to: I still hear your voice in the quiet moments. I still see your shadow when the light hits just right. You told me once that love could outlive death. I'm starting to believe you. And yet, I'm angry, too—angry you left, angry the world took you. I write so I can keep you alive, even if it's only ink on paper."

By the time she finished, Joey's chest ached. He reached across the table and took her hand. "Janet…"

Her smile was faint, fragile. "Now you know."

After that night, the letters became a quiet presence between them. She never showed him more, but sometimes he caught her at her desk, pen moving furiously, tears streaking her face. Other times she would slip an envelope into a drawer as soon as he entered, as if guarding a part of herself she wasn't ready to share.

Joey tried not to pry, but curiosity gnawed at him. What ghosts haunted her words? Who were the goodbyes left unsaid?

One night, after she had fallen asleep beside him, Joey lay awake, staring at the ceiling. He thought about the letters, about the weight Janet carried, and he felt torn between the desire to protect her and the fear that he never could.

Their love, meanwhile, grew fiercer. Days blurred into nights, their stolen moments thick with passion and longing. Yet always, underneath, was the sense that time was fragile, slipping through their fingers.

"Why do you look at me like that?" Janet asked one evening, her head resting on his chest.

"Like what?"

"Like you're memorizing me."

Joey kissed her hair. "Maybe I am."

She lifted her head, her smile tinged with sadness. "Don't. Memories hurt more than silence."

Her words lodged in him, but he didn't argue. Instead, he kissed her again, as though the act itself could keep her anchored.

One day, Joey arrived at her apartment to find her sitting cross-legged on the floor, surrounded by open letters. Dozens of them, strewn like fallen leaves. She looked up, startled, then quickly began gathering them.

"You weren't supposed to see this," she whispered.

Joey knelt, gently stopping her hands. "It's okay. You don't have to hide from me."

Her eyes filled with tears. "But I do. Because if you read these… you'll see all the broken parts. And maybe you'll walk away."

"I won't."

"You don't know that."

Joey cupped her face, forcing her to look at him. "Then show me. Show me your broken parts. I'd rather know the truth than lose you to secrets."

For a long moment, she searched his face. Then, with trembling hands, she picked up one of the letters and pressed it into his palm.

"Read," she whispered.

The letter was dated two years ago.

"To the man I loved and lost: I wish I could hate you. I wish I could erase the way your laughter sounded, the way your touch lingered. But I can't. You're gone, and yet you're everywhere. Sometimes I think about following you, just to end the ache. But then I wonder if I'm meant to stay, to carry both our lives on my shoulders. I don't know if I'm strong enough. But I keep writing, because it's all I can do."

Joey's hands shook as he finished. The rawness, the despair, the intimacy of her grief—it was overwhelming.

"Janet…" His voice cracked. "You don't have to carry this alone."

She collapsed against him then, sobbing into his chest, her body trembling. "But I do. Because the moment I let someone in, I risk losing them too. And I can't survive that again."

Joey held her tightly, his own tears blurring his vision. "You won't lose me," he whispered, though even as he said it, he felt the fragility of the promise.

That night, they made love with a desperation neither had voiced before. It wasn't just passion—it was pleading, an attempt to carve permanence into something fleeting. Every kiss tasted of salt and longing, every touch a vow neither of them knew how to keep.

Afterward, as Janet lay curled against him, she whispered, "If anything ever happens to me, promise you'll remember me like this. Not as broken. Not as a ghost."

Joey kissed her forehead, his heart breaking. "I'll remember you as mine."

Her smile was small, trembling. "That's all I want."

From then on, Joey understood that their love was a house built on fragile ground. The letters were her confessions, her bleeding wounds, and though she shared pieces with him, he knew there were depths she would never reveal.

But he also knew this: he loved her, wholly, fiercely, even if it meant loving the shadows as much as the light.

And if the letters were the only way she could speak her truths, then he would listen—not with his eyes, but with his heart.

Static.

Then, faintly, Janet's voice. Broken, trembling.

"Joey… if you get this…" A pause, ragged breathing. "I don't know if it's safe anymore. He's—"

The recording cut off with a sharp crackle.

Joey's blood went cold.

He tried calling her immediately, but the line rang without answer. He texted, no reply. His chest tightened with every minute that passed in silence. Finally, after nearly an hour, she responded.

"Sorry. Fell asleep. Bad dream. Don't worry."

But he couldn't believe it. He called again, and this time she picked up, her voice soft, almost casual.

"Hey," she said.

"Don't 'hey' me," Joey snapped. "What was that voicemail?"

"What voicemail?"

"The one you left me. You sounded—" He broke off, struggling to breathe. "You sounded terrified."

Silence. Then, slowly: "Joey… I didn't call you tonight."

His stomach dropped. "But it was your number."

"I swear, it wasn't me."

The line hummed with silence, and for a moment Joey wondered if the world had tilted beneath him.

"Maybe it was a glitch," Janet offered weakly. But even she didn't sound convinced.

From that night on, things began to unravel.

The voicemails kept coming, sporadic, unpredictable. Always from Janet's number, always in the dead of night. Sometimes it was only static. Sometimes it was her voice, fractured, filled with fear.

"…he knows…"

"…I can't run anymore…"

"…Joey, I love you, but if I disappear—"

Each message left Joey shaken, sleepless, his heart pounding with dread. When he asked Janet about them, she insisted she hadn't called, that she hadn't left those words.

"Do you think I'd keep something like this from you?" she pleaded, her eyes wet.

He wanted to believe her. But the messages felt too real, too raw, to be nothing.

One night, after another haunting voicemail, Joey couldn't take it anymore. He went to Janet's apartment unannounced, banging on her door until she opened.

Her eyes were red from crying, her hands trembling.

"What happened?" Joey demanded.

She shook her head, pulling him inside. "You shouldn't be here."

"What do you mean? Janet, talk to me!"

But instead of answering, she clung to him, her body shaking. "Just hold me," she whispered. "Please. Just for tonight."

Joey wrapped his arms around her, but even as he did, the voicemail echoed in his mind. If I disappear…

Their intimacy grew heavier, tinged with fear. They clung to each other with desperation, as though each embrace might be their last. Joey found himself memorizing her touch, her voice, the way her breath hitched when he kissed her.

But beneath it all was a gnawing question: who was the "he" in the voicemail? And how close was he to taking her away?

The answer came sooner than Joey expected.

One night, after Janet had finally fallen into a restless sleep beside him, Joey's phone buzzed again. Another voicemail. Hands trembling, he pressed play.

This time, the voice wasn't Janet's.

It was male. Deep, cold.

"You can't protect her, Joey. She was mine long before she was yours. And soon, she'll be mine again."

The message ended in silence.

Joey's blood turned to ice.

The next morning, he confronted Janet.

Her face went pale as he replayed the voicemail for her. Tears welled in her eyes, and she shook her head violently. "No. No, it can't be."

"Who is he?" Joey demanded.

She pressed her hands to her face, sobbing. "I thought—I thought I was free of him."

"Who?"

She lowered her hands, her voice a whisper. "Elias."

The name struck Joey like a blade. Elias—the painter, the ghost from his past, the man who had smirked in the gallery, who had spoken of blood and beauty as if they were interchangeable.

Janet's body trembled as she whispered, "He won't let me go."

Joey pulled her into his arms, his mind racing. The voicemails weren't accidents. They weren't glitches. They were warnings.

And now, the shadows in Janet's smile made sense.

She hadn't just been haunted by ghosts of memory. She was being hunted.

CHAPTER 7: THE MAN IN THE SHADOWS

The city at night was a living thing. Its veins glowed with the pulse of neon, its heartbeat thudded with distant bass lines, its breath whispered in the wind that curled between alleys. But to Joey, walking hand in hand with Janet down a rain-slick street, the city felt suffocating. Every shadow stretched too far, every footstep echoed too long.

Janet clung to his arm, her shoulders tense beneath her coat. She'd said little since the voicemail, only glancing over her shoulder as though expecting someone to emerge from the darkness.

"Janet," Joey whispered, pulling her closer. "Talk to me. I need you to trust me."

"I do trust you," she murmured. Her fingers dug into his sleeve. "That's why I'm terrified."

They turned the corner toward her apartment. That was when Joey felt it—the unmistakable sensation of being watched. His pulse quickened. He stopped abruptly, scanning the street. A man leaned against a lamppost half a block away, the glow of a cigarette briefly illuminating his face.

Elias.

Even at a distance, Joey knew him. The slick hair, the predator's stillness, the faint curl of a smirk.

Janet stiffened. "It's him," she whispered.

Joey stepped instinctively in front of her. "Stay behind me."

Elias took one last drag on his cigarette, flicked it into the gutter, and began walking toward them. His steps were unhurried, deliberate. The kind of walk that said: I own this moment.

When he finally stopped a few feet away, Elias's eyes gleamed in the half-light. "Joey. Janet. Out for a stroll? How domestic."

Joey's jaw tightened. "Stay away from her."

Elias tilted his head, amused. "Away? But Janet and I… we go back, don't we, love?"

Janet's grip on Joey's arm tightened, her body trembling. "Don't call me that."

"Oh, but you liked it once," Elias said softly, his smile twisting. "You liked everything once. The letters, the promises, the nights you swore you'd never leave."

Joey's stomach turned. "You're sick."

Elias chuckled. "No, Joey. I'm an artist. And she was my masterpiece until you smeared yourself across the canvas."

Joey lunged forward, but Janet pulled him back, her voice sharp with fear. "Don't, Joey. That's what he wants."

Elias's smile widened. "Listen to her. She knows I always get what I want in the end."

Then, without another word, he stepped back into the shadows. One blink, and he was gone.

Inside Janet's apartment, the silence was unbearable. She paced the floor, her hands tangled in her hair.

"He won't stop," she whispered. "He'll destroy everything just to prove he can."

Joey caught her wrists, forcing her to meet his gaze. "Then we fight. Together."

Tears streamed down her cheeks. "You don't know what he's capable of."

"Then tell me. Please. Don't shut me out."

She sank onto the couch, trembling. "Elias was… everything once. He made me feel seen, wanted. But it wasn't love. It was control. Every word, every touch, he twisted into something poisonous. I left, but leaving him was like tearing off my own skin. He told me I'd never escape."

Joey knelt before her, his hands cupping hers. "You did escape. You're here. With me. He's nothing but noise now."

Janet's lips trembled. "Noise doesn't stalk you in the night. Noise doesn't leave voicemails."

Joey kissed her knuckles, his voice fierce. "Then let him watch. Let him whisper. He won't take you back. Not while I breathe."

For the first time that night, a faint smile flickered across her face. But her eyes still glistened with fear.

That night, they didn't sleep. They clung to each other in bed, the city's hum outside their window. Every creak of the building, every distant horn felt like Elias reaching for them.

Janet buried her face against Joey's chest. "If he takes me…"

"Don't," Joey interrupted. "Don't even say it."

"But if he does," she insisted, her voice breaking, "remember that I loved you. Remember that I chose you."

Joey's heart fractured. He kissed her fiercely, desperately. "He won't. Do you hear me, Janet? He won't."

They made love like it was their last chance, every touch both a promise and a plea. When dawn finally bled into the room, Joey lay awake, watching her sleep, vowing silently that Elias would never have her again.

But vows were fragile things.

The next evening, Joey walked Janet home from the café. As they neared her building, he froze. A canvas leaned against her door, wrapped in brown paper.

Janet's face went pale. "Don't touch it."

But Joey was already tearing it open, fury boiling in his veins.

The painting inside was unmistakable: Janet, painted in Elias's unmistakable style. Her face, her body, rendered with haunting precision. But crimson streaks ran down the canvas, pooling at her feet like blood.

At the bottom, scrawled in thick, black paint: She belongs to me.

Janet's knees buckled, and Joey caught her before she collapsed. She was shaking violently, her breath coming in short gasps.

"He's inside my head again," she whispered.

Joey pulled her close, his rage burning hotter than fear. "Then I'll rip him out."

That night, Joey burned the painting in the alley behind her apartment. Flames licked the air, devouring Elias's twisted vision, but the stench of smoke did nothing to ease the dread that clung to them.

From the shadows across the street, Joey swore he saw the faint glow of a cigarette.

And the shape of a man watching.

Always watching.

CHAPTER 8: A SILENCE TOO LOUD

Silence used to be Janet's refuge. She had always sought it—the hush of early mornings, the stillness of candlelit nights, the quiet places where her thoughts could bleed into ink. But lately, silence had become something else. Something suffocating.

Because silence now meant he was near.

Joey noticed it first in the café. One minute, Janet was laughing at something he'd said, her smile tugging at his heart the way it always did. Then, without warning, she froze. The laughter died in her throat. The café's bustle seemed to fade, leaving a ringing quiet in its wake.

Joey leaned forward. "What is it?"

Her eyes darted toward the window. Across the street, a man stood half-shrouded in shadow. Cigarette glowing. Watching.

Joey shot to his feet, but by the time he reached the door, the man was gone.

When he returned, Janet was trembling, her face pale. "Do you hear it?" she whispered.

"Hear what?"

"The silence. That's how I know he's close."

That night, Janet insisted on staying at Joey's apartment. She curled into him on the couch, her body tense, her eyes flicking toward every creak of the building.

Joey stroked her hair, murmuring, "He can't touch you here. Not with me."

But she didn't answer. Instead, she closed her eyes as if willing herself to believe him.

Later, when she finally drifted into sleep, Joey sat awake, listening. The silence in the apartment seemed alive. It pressed against him, thick and heavy, carrying the weight of unseen eyes.

At 2 a.m., his phone buzzed. Another voicemail.

Hands shaking, Joey played it.

Static. Then, faintly, Janet's voice.

"Joey… please… don't let him—"

The message cut off with a scream.

Joey's chest tightened as he stared at Janet sleeping beside him, her breath steady, oblivious. The scream still rang in his ears.

The next day, Joey confronted Elias outside the gallery where his new exhibition was being advertised.

"Stay away from her," Joey growled, shoving Elias against the brick wall.

Elias only smiled, unbothered. "Touching. Do you think she's yours because you hold her at night? Because she whispers your name instead of mine?"

"She's not yours."

"Oh, but she is. She always will be. You see, Joey…" Elias leaned closer, his voice a hiss. "…she loved me first. And first love—real love—it stains. It doesn't wash away, no matter how hard you scrub."

Joey slammed him harder against the wall, but Elias only chuckled, unfazed. “Careful. The louder you get, the more she’ll realize how weak you really are.”

Joey released him with disgust, shoving him away. “If you come near her again—”

Elias smirked, brushing dust from his jacket. “You’ll what? Play me a sad song on your piano? Write her a sonnet? You’re not built for war, Joey. But I am.”

The words sank like poison.

That night, Janet sat at Joey’s piano, her fingers resting on the keys though she didn’t play. The lamplight cast her in gold, but her eyes were distant, haunted.

“Do you ever wonder,” she whispered, “if silence can kill?”

Joey frowned. "What do you mean?"

"When the world goes too quiet. When everything feels… paused. Like the moment before lightning strikes." She shuddered. "That's what it feels like now. Like we're waiting for the thunder."

Joey wrapped his arms around her from behind, resting his chin on her shoulder. "Then let it strike. We'll survive it. Together."

Her hand covered his, squeezing tightly. "Promise?"

"I promise."

But even as he said it, Joey wondered if promises were strong enough to hold back a storm.

The storm came two nights later.

They were walking home from the café again when the streetlights flickered out, plunging the block into sudden darkness. Janet gasped, clutching Joey's arm.

"Stay close," he murmured, guiding her quickly down the street. His heart pounded in his chest.

From the alley came the sound of footsteps. Slow. Deliberate.

"Joey…" Janet's voice trembled.

He turned sharply, scanning the shadows. For a moment, nothing. Then—a shape. Tall. Familiar. Cigarette glow flaring.

Elias.

Joey shoved Janet behind him. "Run."

But Janet didn't move. She was frozen, her eyes wide, locked on Elias.

Elias stepped forward, his voice calm, almost tender. "Janet. Come home."

Something inside her snapped. She screamed, a raw, broken sound, before bolting down the street.

Joey chased after her, his lungs burning. He caught her at the corner, grabbing her shoulders. "Janet, stop! It's me!"

She collapsed against him, sobbing uncontrollably. "I can't… I can't do this anymore."

Joey held her tight, whispering over and over, "You're safe. You're safe." But his own voice shook. Because for the first time, he wasn't sure it was true.

Back in the apartment, Janet sat trembling on the bed, clutching a letter in her hands. Joey recognized the twine wrapping, the familiar scrawl of her private confessions.

"What's that?" he asked gently.

She lifted it with shaking fingers. "A goodbye. I wrote it months ago. For you. In case he ever found me."

Joey's stomach twisted. "Don't say that. Don't even think it."

Her tears spilled freely now. "I need you to know—if he takes me, if silence swallows me whole—I loved you more than I ever loved him. More than I ever thought I could love anyone."

Joey fell to his knees before her, tearing the letter from her hands. He ripped it to shreds, the paper fluttering like snow to the floor.

"No goodbyes," he whispered fiercely. "Not from you. Not to me. We fight until the end."

Janet stared at him, broken and beautiful, before pulling him into a kiss that tasted of desperation and salt.

And in that kiss, Joey understood the truth: Elias wasn't just in the shadows anymore. He was inside them, breaking them apart piece by piece.

CHAPTER 9: THE NIGHT IT ALL FELL APART

The night began almost beautifully.

Rain had washed the city clean, leaving the streets gleaming under the glow of streetlights. Joey and Janet sat by the window of his apartment, sharing wine and watching droplets race down the glass. For a few fleeting hours, it felt like the world outside didn't exist.

Janet laughed softly, curling against him. "For once, it's quiet."

Joey kissed her temple. "The good kind of quiet."

She nodded, eyes closing as though savoring the stillness. He thought, not for the first time, that maybe they had beaten the darkness. That maybe Elias was nothing more than a fading nightmare.

But hope, Joey would learn, was fragile.

At 11:47 p.m., the phone rang.

Not Joey's phone. The landline. The one no one ever called.

Janet stiffened in his arms, her body going rigid.

"Don't answer it," she whispered.

The phone rang again. And again. Each chime felt sharper, cutting through the silence. Finally, Joey rose, jaw tight, and snatched up the receiver.

Static hissed. Then, faintly, a man's voice.

"Enjoying the quiet, Joey?"

Joey's grip tightened on the phone. "Elias."

Janet gasped behind him.

Elias chuckled. "She looks beautiful tonight. That dress. That glass of wine in her hand. Shame it'll all be red soon."

Joey slammed the phone down, his heart pounding. He turned to Janet, who stood frozen, her wineglass trembling in her hand.

"He's here," she whispered.

Joey rushed to the window. Across the street, under the broken halo of a flickering streetlight, Elias stood. His pale face tilted upward, cigarette glowing like a sinister star.

Joey yanked the curtains shut. "We're leaving."

"Where?" Janet asked, panic in her eyes.

"Anywhere but here."

But it was already too late.

A crash shattered the air — the sound of glass breaking. Joey spun toward the kitchen. A brick lay on the floor, surrounded by shards. Attached to it with tape was an envelope.

Janet's scream pierced the silence.

Joey tore it open with shaking hands. Inside was a single sheet of paper, painted in crimson strokes:

TONIGHT, SHE BLEEDS.

Chaos followed.

Joey grabbed Janet's hand and pulled her toward the door, but the hallway outside was dark — the power cut. Their footsteps echoed in the oppressive silence as they fled down the stairwell.

Halfway down, Janet froze. "Do you hear that?"

Joey stopped. The sound was faint at first — the scrape of a shoe against concrete. Then another.

Someone was following them.

"Keep moving," Joey urged, pulling her faster.

They burst out into the alley behind the building, rain pelting their faces. The city felt deserted, the streets too quiet, the silence unnatural.

Janet clung to him, breath ragged. "He's here."

Joey scanned the shadows, fury burning hotter than fear. "Elias! Show yourself!"

For a long, unbearable moment, nothing. Then, from the darkness: a low chuckle.

"You make this too easy."

Elias stepped into the dim light, his expression calm, almost serene. He looked like he had all the time in the world.

"Janet," he said softly, like a lover greeting his muse. "Come home."

"No!" Janet screamed, her voice cracking. "I'm not yours!"

Joey moved in front of her, fists clenched. "You'll never touch her again."

Elias smirked. "Brave. Useless, but brave."

Then everything happened at once.

Elias lunged.

Joey shoved Janet aside and met him head-on, the two men colliding in the rain-slick alley. Fists flew, grunts filled the night. Joey fought with every ounce of rage he had, but Elias was stronger, fueled by obsession.

A punch landed against Joey's ribs, sending him staggering. Elias's laughter echoed, cruel and sharp.

"You can't save her!" Elias roared. "She's already mine!"

"Not anymore!" Joey growled, swinging back.

Behind them, Janet screamed. She had grabbed the fallen brick, her hands trembling as she raised it. "Stay away from him!"

For a heartbeat, Elias's eyes flicked toward her. It was enough. Joey lunged, tackling him to the ground. They grappled, rain mixing with blood, each man desperate to win.

But then—steel glinted in the dark.

Elias pulled a knife from his jacket, his grin feral.

Joey's heart stopped.

"Joey!" Janet shrieked.

The blade slashed. Pain seared Joey's side, hot and blinding. He staggered, clutching the wound, his vision swimming.

"No!" Janet's voice broke as she hurled the brick, striking Elias's shoulder. He stumbled, cursing, but recovered quickly, his knife gleaming.

Janet rushed to Joey's side, tears streaming. "Stay with me!"

Elias stepped closer, his smile cold. "Beautiful. You'll die in his arms. Just as I dreamed."

In the chaos, Janet did the only thing she could think of. She grabbed Joey's phone from his pocket, fumbling to dial emergency services. But Elias was too fast. He lunged, knocking it from her hands.

"Enough games," he hissed. "You're mine, Janet. You always were."

And with those words, he drove the knife forward.

Janet gasped, the world tilting around her as the blade pierced her chest. Her scream was swallowed by silence, the city holding its breath.

Joey's roar tore through the night. "NO!"

He threw himself at Elias, rage and grief turning him into something unrecognizable. The two men crashed against the alley wall, struggling for the knife. Blood smeared the bricks, the rain washing it down in crimson rivers.

In the struggle, the blade turned. A sharp pain exploded in Joey's chest. His breath hitched, the world spinning.

Janet's voice, faint and broken, reached him. "Joey…"

Their eyes met. Her lips curved in a trembling smile even as blood stained them.

"I love you," she whispered.

"I love you too," he rasped, before darkness swallowed him.

The alley was silent once more. Too silent.

A silence too loud.

And in that silence, everything fell apart.

CHAPTER 10: LOVE IN THE MORGUE

The morgue was colder than Joey ever imagined.

Even in death, he thought, the world should've given Janet warmth. She had lived like fire — fierce, bright, untamable — and now she lay still beneath a sterile white sheet.

Joey wasn't sure how long he'd been standing there. Minutes, hours. Time didn't exist here. Only the quiet hum of fluorescent lights and the hollow echo of his heartbeat.

His hand trembled as he reached out, brushing the edge of the sheet back. There she was. Pale. Perfect. As if sleeping.

"Janet…" His voice cracked. "I promised I wouldn't let him take you. I failed."

His chest burned where the knife had carved through him. He could still feel the warmth of her blood mixing with his, still hear her final whisper. I love you.

And then darkness.

Yet somehow, he was here. Alive, though shattered. Staring at the woman who had been his everything.

The coroner had tried to stop him. "Family only," the man had said.

Joey had looked him in the eyes and whispered, "She was my family."

Something in his voice must have carried enough truth, because the coroner stepped aside.

Now Joey stood alone in the morgue, drowning in grief.

He bent down, pressing his lips to Janet's cool forehead. "Do you hear me, love? I'd trade places with you a thousand times. I'd bleed again and again if it meant you could breathe once more."

His tears fell freely, landing on her still hand. He wrapped his fingers around hers, willing warmth into them. "This isn't the end. You don't get to leave me like this."

He thought he was imagining it at first.

The faintest whisper in the silence. A voice, soft and familiar.

"I'm still here, Joey."

He froze. The room seemed to tilt.

"Janet?" His voice shook.

Silence again. Then, clearer: "Don't let go."

Joey's heart pounded. He clutched her hand tighter, tears blurring his vision. "I won't. I'll never let go."

And then — the strangest thing. He felt it. The faintest squeeze.

For hours, Joey sat there, speaking softly to her. About the songs he never finished, about the mornings she'd stolen coffee before kissing him, about the dreams they hadn't yet lived.

And though her lips never moved, he swore he could hear her responses, faint as breath, threaded into the silence.

"I loved those mornings."

"Don't let him steal our story."

"Promise me this isn't goodbye."

By the time the coroner returned, Joey's face was wet, his voice hoarse. But his grip on Janet's hand was iron.

The coroner frowned. "Sir, visiting hours—"

"She's not gone," Joey interrupted, his voice low, fierce. "Not yet."

The coroner hesitated, as though sensing something sacred, then quietly left him there.

Night fell. The morgue emptied. The city outside moved on, oblivious.

But Joey stayed.

At some point, he lay down beside Janet on the steel table, pulling the sheet back just enough to wrap an arm around her. It was cold, but it was hers.

And in that fragile space between waking and dreams, he felt her warmth again.

Not in the room. Not in the world. But somewhere deeper.

"I'm waiting, Joey," her voice whispered in his mind. "When the time is right, find me."

Joey pressed his forehead against hers, eyes closed. "I'll find you. Even if I have to tear heaven apart to reach you."

And in that promise, he finally slept.

When morning came, the staff found him still there, holding her. They tried to move him, but his grip was unyielding, his body limp from exhaustion.

To them, it looked like madness.

To Joey, it was love.

Love in the morgue.

CHAPTER 11: THE CONFESSION

The courtroom was smaller than Joey expected.

After everything — the blood, the screams, the endless nights — he thought justice would unfold in some vast, echoing chamber. But instead, it was four beige walls, rows of creaking benches, and a handful of strangers who would never understand the gravity of what had been stolen.

At the front, chained and smirking, sat Elias.

Joey's stomach twisted. He'd imagined this moment a hundred times — the man in shadows finally dragged into the light. But nothing could prepare him for the calm, almost smug expression on Elias's face.

The prosecutor cleared his throat. "Elias Marrow, you stand accused of stalking, harassment, and the murders of Janet Ellis and Joseph Hale."

A murmur rippled through the room. Joey's fists clenched. Murders. Plural. His name among them.

And yet, here he was. Watching. Listening. Somewhere between the living and the dead.

Janet's voice lingered in him still, soft as a memory: "Find me when the time is right."

The trial began with evidence — the letters, the voicemails, the painting defaced with blood-red strokes. Joey listened as they described Elias's obsession, his descent into possession masquerading as art.

But none of it mattered when Elias finally spoke.

They had barely begun questioning him when he leaned into the microphone, his eyes scanning the room as though searching for someone unseen.

"Janet," he whispered.

Joey's blood boiled.

"She was mine," Elias said louder, his voice trembling with something between fury and longing. "Do you understand? She wasn't a woman. She wasn't flesh and bone. She was my canvas. My muse. The only thing that gave my life meaning."

Gasps echoed through the room. The judge banged her gavel. "Mr. Marrow, control yourself."

But Elias didn't stop. His gaze burned, unblinking, as if Janet herself stood before him.

"She let me in," he hissed. "She let me see her soul. Do you know what that does to a man? To touch perfection, to shape it, to own it — and then to have it stolen?"

Joey's chest tightened. He wanted to leap across the aisle, to break Elias's chains with his bare hands just so he could kill him again.

Instead, he sat frozen, listening.

The defense attorney buried his face in his hands. "Elias, please—"

"No," Elias snapped, slamming his palms on the table. "You want the truth? Fine. I killed her. I killed him. And I'd do it again. Because if I can't have her, no one can."

The words hung in the air like smoke, thick and suffocating.

The courtroom erupted. The judge shouted for order. But Joey heard nothing beyond that confession, echoing like a death knell.

I killed her. I killed him.

And suddenly, Joey wasn't in the courtroom anymore.

He was back in the alley. Rain on his skin. Janet's scream splitting the night. The knife flashing. Her blood mixing with his.

The silence that followed.

When Joey blinked again, he was alone. Not in the courtroom. Not in the alley.

Somewhere in between.

A vast, endless space of white light.

And standing before him — Janet.

She was radiant, unscarred, smiling through her tears.

"Joey," she whispered.

His knees buckled. He fell into her arms, holding her as though the world might tear them apart again. "You're here. You're real."

"I've always been here," she said softly. "Even in the morgue. Even in the silence. I never left you."

He kissed her, desperate, tasting warmth instead of blood this time. "He confessed, Janet. He admitted it. The world knows what he did."

Janet's eyes shone. "Then it's over."

Joey shook his head. "Not until I know you're safe."

She cupped his face, her smile tender. "I'm safe now. And soon… so will you."

The light dimmed. The courtroom returned. Elias was still ranting, screaming Janet's name, spitting madness into the air. But Joey barely heard him.

Because for the first time since the alley, Joey felt peace.

The confession was made. The truth was free.

And Janet was waiting.

CHAPTER 12: OUR FOREVER, IN ANOTHER LIFE

The first thing Joey felt was warmth.

Not the sterile chill of the morgue, not the damp cold of rain-slick alleys, but a warmth that seemed to seep into his very soul. He opened his eyes slowly, breath catching in his throat.

He was standing in a field. Endless and golden, the grass bending in a wind that didn't sting, a sky that glowed with hues of violet and gold. Everything shimmered, alive with a light that didn't burn but embraced.

And then — her laughter.

Joey spun, heart pounding.

There she was. Janet.

No bruises. No blood. No trembling from fear. She was radiant, her hair catching the sunlight, her eyes brighter than he'd ever remembered.

"Janet…" His voice broke as tears blurred his vision.

She smiled, stepping toward him. "Took you long enough."

He ran. She ran. And when they collided, it was like the world righted itself. He crushed her against him, breathing her in, his tears wetting her skin.

"I thought I lost you," he whispered.

"You did," she murmured against his lips. "But only for a moment. Death couldn't keep us apart. Nothing ever could."

They sat together in the grass, fingers entwined, as though no time had passed. Joey couldn't stop staring at her, afraid she might vanish again.

"This place," he said softly. "Where are we?"

She rested her head against his shoulder. "A place beyond fear. Beyond silence. Call it heaven. Call it forever. All I know is — it's ours."

He kissed her hair, eyes closing. For the first time in what felt like lifetimes, he exhaled without pain.

"You waited for me."

"I promised I would." She lifted his hand to her lips. "You kept your promise too. You found me."

Time flowed differently here. Or maybe not at all. They walked through meadows, shared kisses beneath skies painted in colors too vivid for earth. They lay together beneath trees that hummed with music instead of leaves, their hearts beating in harmony.

But Joey knew there was one thing left unsaid.

One night, under a canopy of stars that seemed close enough to touch, he whispered, "Janet… I should have protected you. I should have stopped him."

She turned to him, her eyes glistening but steady. "No, Joey. Don't carry that weight. Elias took our lives, but he never touched our love. That was ours, and it always will be."

He swallowed hard, her words soaking into the deepest cracks of his soul. "Then promise me — this time, it's forever."

Janet smiled, luminous. "Forever. In this life, and the next, and every one after."

In the distance, music began to play. Not from any instrument, but from the air itself. Joey recognized it instantly. It was the melody he had once begun at his piano, the one he never finished.

"Do you hear that?" he asked, stunned.

Janet nodded. "It's us. Our song."

They rose together, hand in hand, following the music to the crest of a hill. And there, spread before them, was a horizon alive with light. Not blinding. Inviting.

Joey felt no fear.

Janet squeezed his hand. "Ready?"

"With you? Always."

And together, they stepped forward.

Behind them, the echoes of their earthly love remained — the café where it began, the piano that carried their secrets, the alley where silence screamed. But ahead of them stretched eternity, where no shadows lurked, no knives gleamed, no promises broke.

Only love.

Their love.

In the end, their story wasn't defined by the night it fell apart.

It was defined by the forever that followed.

A forever that belonged to Joey and Janet.

In another life.

Epilogue

Years had passed since that fateful night, yet the echoes of Joey and Janet's love lingered in every quiet corner of the city they once called home. Those who had known them still whispered about the intensity of their bond, the kind of love that didn't fade with absence or time.

In the soft glow of twilight, when the world seemed to hold its breath, it was as if they were there—together, smiling, free from pain, their hearts forever entwined. Love, they realized, was not just for the living. It was eternal, invisible threads connecting souls across worlds, across lifetimes.

Even in silence, even in memory's deepest shadows, Joey and Janet's story remained—a testament to a love that could not be broken.

Author's Note

Thank you for joining me on this journey through love, mystery, and loss. Writing Joey and Janet's story was a reminder that true love often defies logic, defies time, and transcends even the greatest tragedies.

I hope their story stays with you as it does with me, inspiring you to cherish every fleeting moment and believe in the enduring power of love, no matter the circumstances.

— Sahil Shah

"True love endures beyond the confines of time and even death itself."

www.ingramcontent.com/pod-product-compliance
Ingram Content Group UK Ltd.
Pitfield, Milton Keynes, MK11 3LW, UK
UKHW021408190726
13845UKWH00028B/966

9 789334 390117